FIXER

THE ROBOT

Meet Fixer and his friends:

FIXER
THE ROBOT

DUG
THE DIGGER

BULL
THE DOZER

GERTIE
THE GRABBER

→ A FABER PICTURE BOOK ←

FIXER
THE ROBOT

John Kelly

ff

FABER & FABER

Every morning, Fixer robot
trundles up the hill,
To help the other robots as they
dig and push and drill.

"Hello? What's this?"
It's Dug the digger
looking quite dismayed ...

"I've only dug out half this hole,
but broken my new spade!"

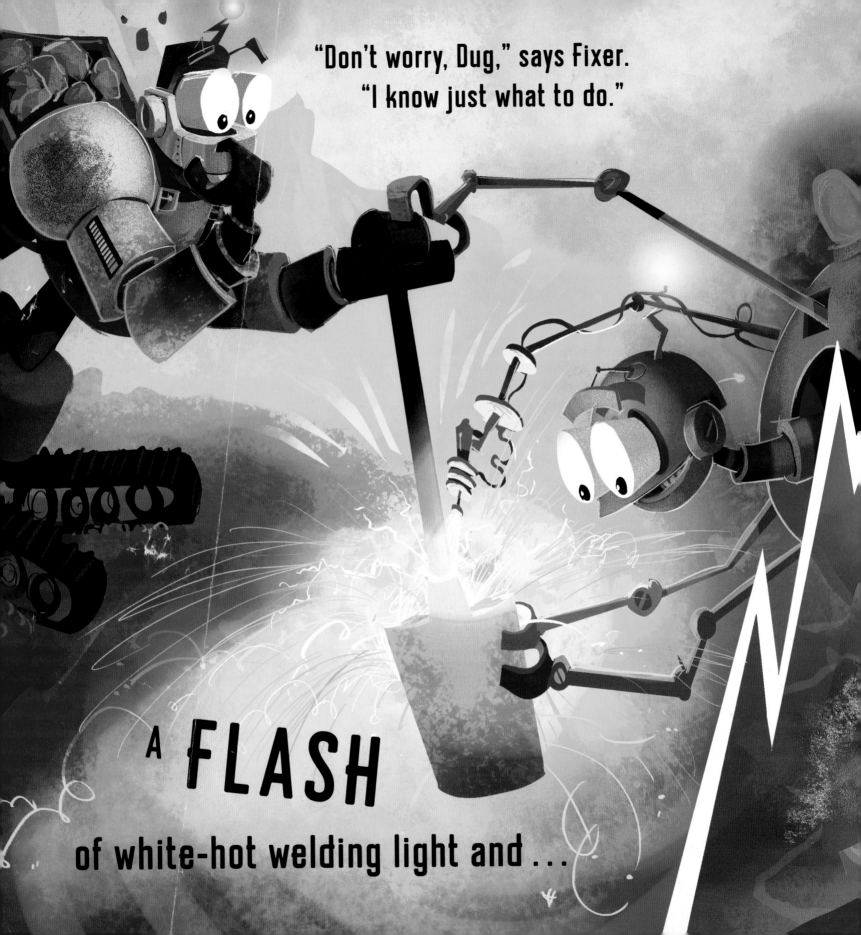

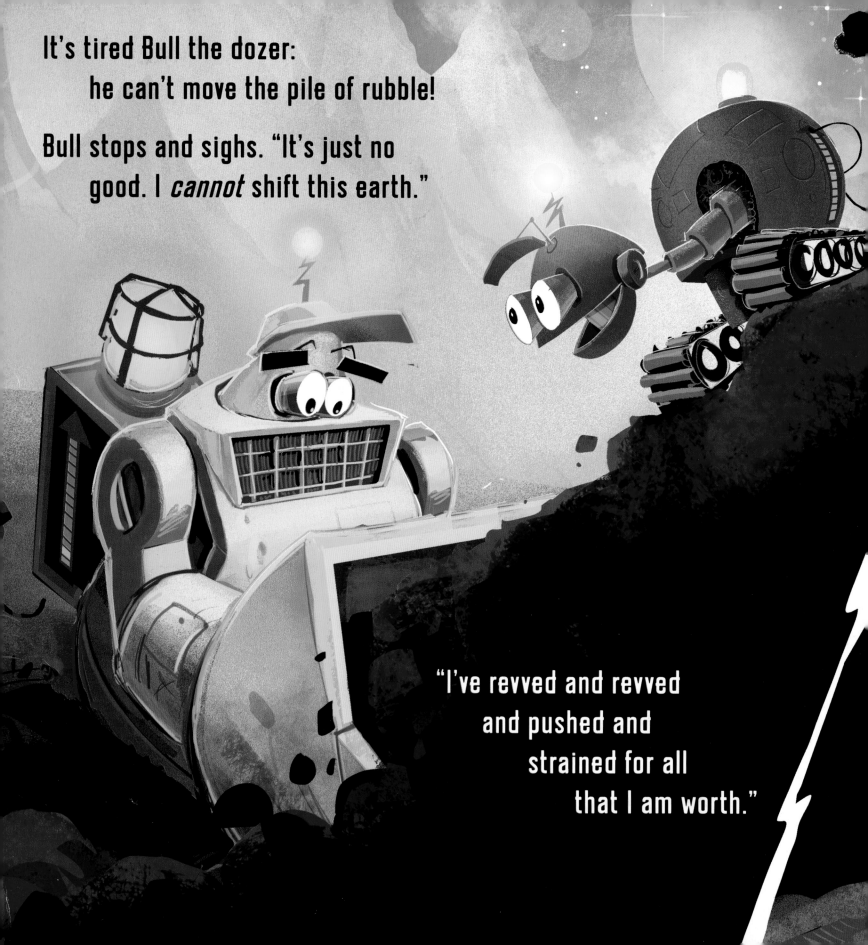

It's tired Bull the dozer:
   he can't move the pile of rubble!

Bull stops and sighs. "It's just no
good. I *cannot* shift this earth."

"I've revved and revved
and pushed and
strained for all
that I am worth."

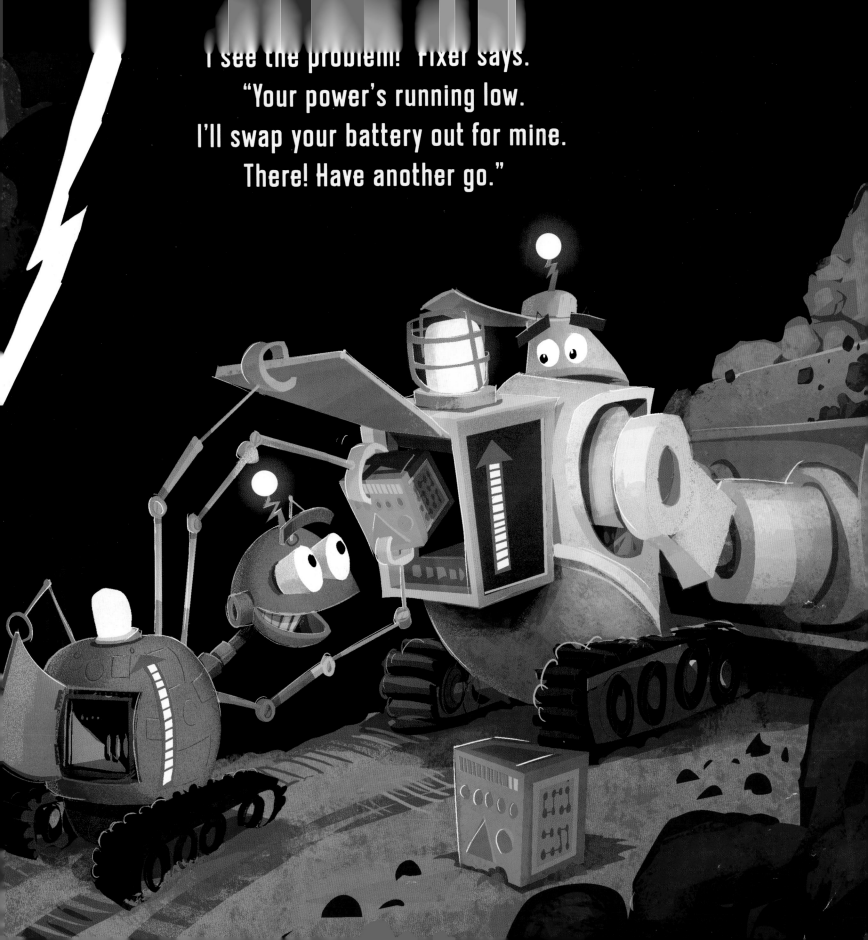

"I see the problem!" Fixer says.
"Your power's running low.
I'll swap your battery out for mine.
There! Have another go."

"I feel like **new**!" says Bull.
"I could lift ten thousand tons!"

"Glad to help,"
Fixer says,
and, tired,
he rolls on.

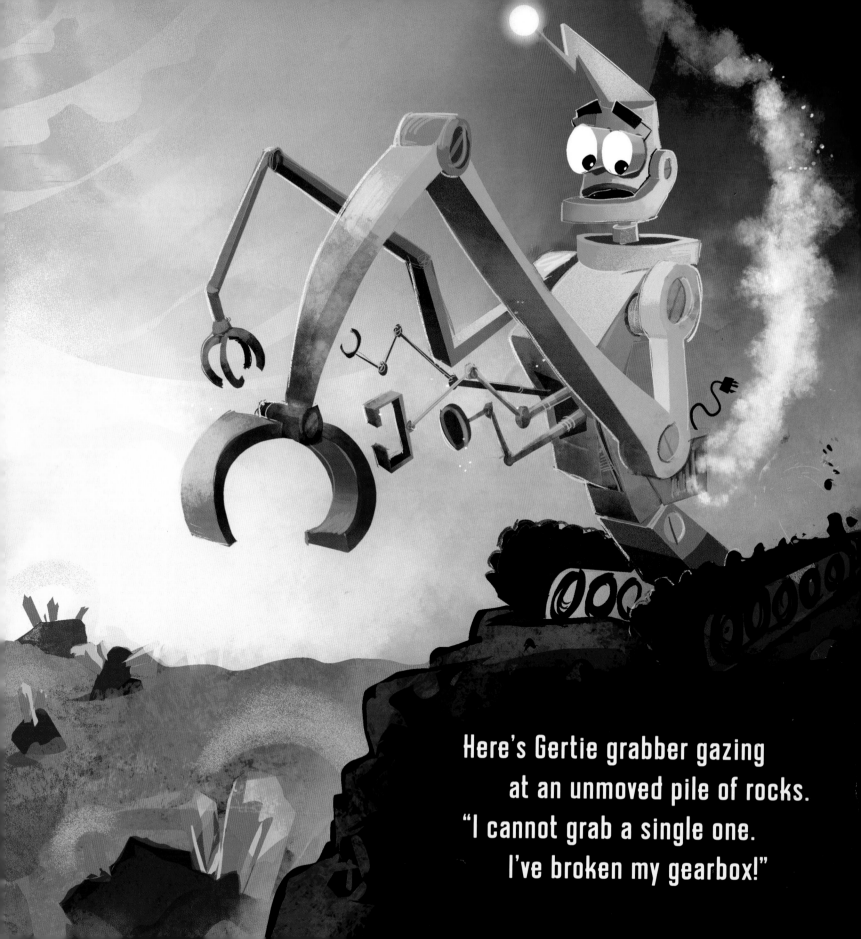

Here's Gertie grabber gazing
at an unmoved pile of rocks.
"I cannot grab a single one.
I've broken my gearbox!"

Have nine," says Fixer, reaching in
and handing her his own.
"First gear is enough for me and
it's time to head back home."

His spare-parts box is empty now,
his battery almost flat.

There's nothing more
to do, he thinks.
Oh well, I'd best head back.

But high above,
a single rock slides
from the mountaintop …
And starts a landslide down the slope
that simply can't be stopped.
"What's that? A storm?"
says Fixer, as he
hears a thunderous

CRASH!

And looks up as the pile of
rocks falls on him with a ...

He wakes to find
  he's buried deep.

His metal treads
  are broken.

His grabber's badly
  twisted and his little
  engine smoking.

He hopes someone will find him,
   but slowly fills with doubt.
His battery fails . . .

         and one . . . by one . . .

                           his little lights . . .

                                    . . . go out.

But luckily for Fixer all his friends are rolling home,
When they find their path is blocked
    by several hundred tons of stone.

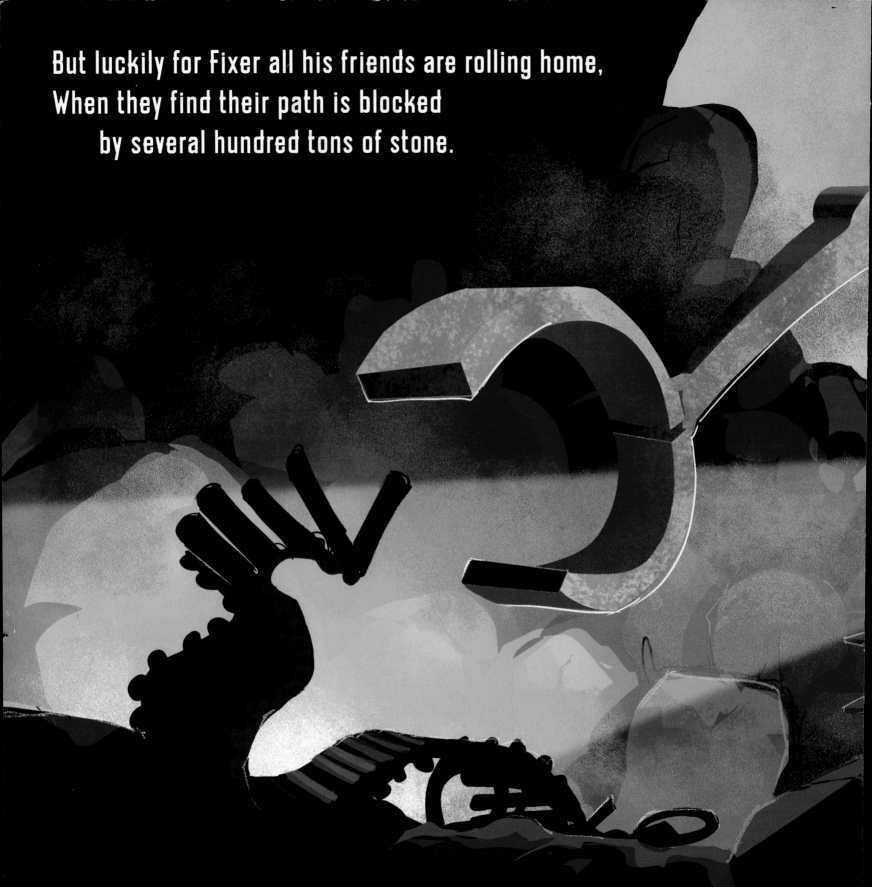

One of Fixer's broken treads
is pinned beneath the rubble.

"Oh no!" cries Dug.

"Quick, help!" says Gertie.
"Fixer is in trouble!"

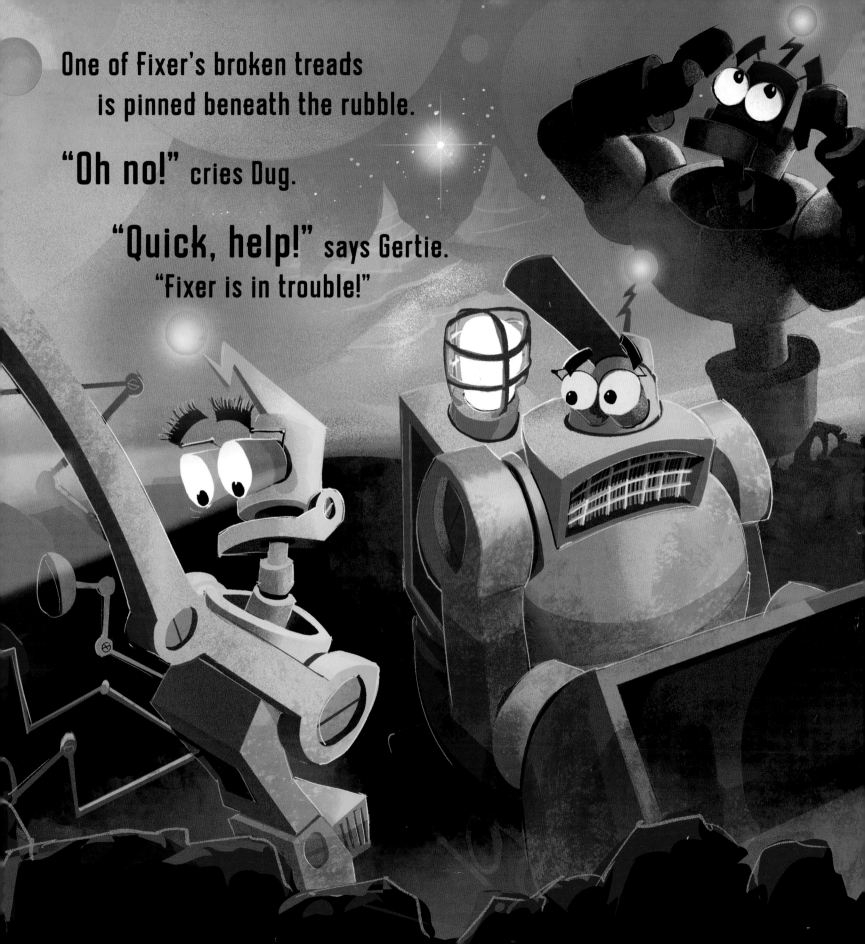

"Don't panic, everybody.
I can shift these rocks," says Bull.
"I'm big and strong and, luckily,
my battery's nearly full."

HEAVE!

Bull heaves the rocks aside
but finds only soil and sand.
"C'mon, Dug!" he cries. "Get over
here and lend a hand."

So Dug the digger's spade bites down
and soil flies through the air.
The hole grows quickly big enough –
they see poor Fixer there.

"He's down too deep,"
says Dug. "I can't reach
him with my spade."

"Then step aside," says
Gertie. "This is just
why I was made!"

Her telescopic grab
extends right down
into the pit.

She s t r e t c h e s, says,
"I'm . . . nearly . . . there . . ."
Then suddenly,
"THAT'S IT!"

"**I'VE GOT HIM!**"
Gertie cries.
And tells the others,
"**Help me pull.**"

So Fixer's dragged
out from the hole
by **Gertie, Dug**
and Bull.

Fixer wakes up back at base
surrounded by his friends.
They smile and say, "We're glad
to see you're finally
on the mend.

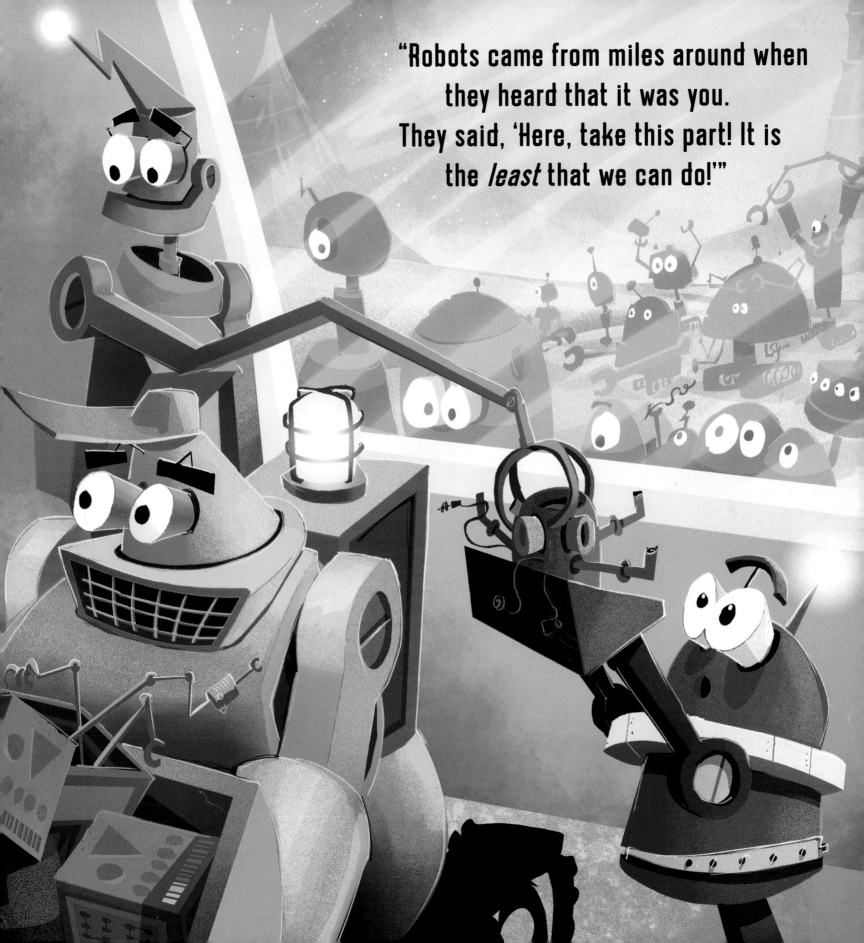

"Robots came from miles around when they heard that it was you. They said, 'Here, take this part! It is the *least* that we can do!'"

So every morning, Fixer robot
trundles up the hill,
To help the other robots as they
dig and push and drill.

FABER & FABER has published
children's books since 1929. Some
of our very first publications included
Old Possum's Book of Practical Cats
by T. S. Eliot starring the now world-
famous Macavity, and *The Iron Man*
by Ted Hughes. Our catalogue
at the time said that "it is by
reading such books that children
learn the difference between the
shoddy and the genuine". We still
believe in the power of reading to
transform children's lives.

First published in the UK in 2018
First published in the USA in 2018
by Faber and Faber Limited
Bloomsbury House, 74–77 Great Russell Street,
London WC1B 3DA

Text and illustration © John Kelly, 2018

HB ISBN 978–0–571–33636–4
PB ISBN 978–0–571–33637–1

Printed in Italy.

10 9 8 7 6 5 4 3 2 1

A CIP record for this book is
available from the British Library.